JUNIOR KROLL,
Esquire

JUNIOR KROLL,
Esquire

Betty Paraskevas

ILLUSTRATED BY
Michael Paraskevas

A Harvest Original
Harcourt Brace & Company
SAN DIEGO   NEW YORK   LONDON

Junior Kroll has been a weekly feature in
Dan's Papers, Bridgehampton, New York,
since June 8, 1990.

Library of Congress Cataloging-in-Publication Data
Paraskevas, Betty.
Junior Kroll, Esquire/by Betty Paraskevas;
illustrated by Michael Paraskevas.—1st ed.
p.   cm.
ISBN 0-15-646572-8
I. Paraskevas, Michael, 1961–   . II. Title.
PS3566.A627J885   1993
811'.54—dc20   93-8040

Designed by Michael Farmer
Printed in the United States of America
First edition
A B C D E

To Rubin Pfeffer

JUNIOR KROLL,
Esquire

Bang That Drum

Junior Kroll beat his little drum
Up and down the driveway
With a *rum-tum-tum!*
Till a neighbor next door
Couldn't take it anymore.
"Fe, fi, fo, fum!
Cut that out or I'll break your drum!"
Junior Kroll with a pail on his head,
Stuck out his tongue, turned around and fled.
Five minutes later with a *rat-ta-tat-tat*,
He was on the march again with his pail for a hat.
Marching at his side, minus his chain,
Was Crazy Max, the Krolls' Great Dane.

Crazy Max

Crazy Max, the Krolls' Great Dane,
Was a time bomb ticking on the end of a chain.
He chewed the drapes, he ate the flowers,
He dug up the lawn, he barked for hours.
They packed his shoe and sent him away
To Fido U. He was back the next day
With a note that read, "Beyond Control."
He'd only answer to Junior Kroll.
Every day Junior walked Max to town.
When they got to the bakery Max sat down;
He wouldn't budge, he'd sit and wait
For his jelly donut on a paper plate.
Yet, as bad as he was, the Krolls' Great Dane
Loved the little boy on the end of his chain.

Junior Kroll and Peas

Junior Kroll said, "Excuse me, please."
Mrs. Kroll said, "Sit down and eat those peas."
He held his nose and slipped back into his chair.
Peas smelled. Peas were dumb. Peas oughta be square.
He thought of rolling the peas that fall
Off everyone's fork into one big ball.
He'd push that ball and he'd never stop
Till he pushed it over a mountaintop.
Whoa! Look at it go!
Heading straight for the road below.
He conjured up a gruesome scene.
A truck skids on that gooky green.
It flips on its side dumping a load
Of nice fresh peas all over the road.
Junior's fantasy was interrupted
And his integrity sadly corrupted
When Mom brought in the Key Lime Pie.
Junior heaved a sorrowful sigh
And slipped the peas to Crazy Max
Under the table, begging for snacks.
Later Mrs. Kroll found the peas.
Tapping her foot she asked, "What are these?"
"They must have rolled off my fork," Junior said.
Crazy Max sniffed and turned his head,
As if to say with his nose in the air,
"Peas smell. Peas are dumb. Peas oughta be square!"

A Visit to the Eye Doctor

Junior Kroll announced that he wanted to wear
Glasses for a touch of savoir faire.
Mom and Dad did not agree,
So Junior plotted to make them see.
He'd put down his book, and his eyes would close.
Then he'd sigh and pinch the bridge of his nose.
When Mom and Dad didn't take the hint,
Junior Kroll began to squint.
He never gave up. And one night as they ate,
Junior stuck his nose one inch from his plate.
"Eureka," he said, "what are these?
I've never seen such tiny peas."
Mom and Dad were enjoying the show
And wondering just how far he'd go.
When Junior played the *Dark Victory* scene
Better than Davis on the silver screen,
Mrs. Kroll decided it was time to reach
Dr. Lamonsoff in Westhampton Beach.
The doctor said to send Junior on down.
So Junior and Max walked to town.
When Dr. Lamonsoff examined Junior's eyes,
He said they were fine but he did sympathize
With anyone desiring a little savoir faire.
Then he reached into a drawer and brought out a pair
Of specs with lenses of window glass.
He agreed they added a touch of class.
Junior gazed in the mirror and immediately
Blossomed into maturity.
For three days he wore them. Then, Mrs. Kroll said,
On the fourth day she found them under his bed.

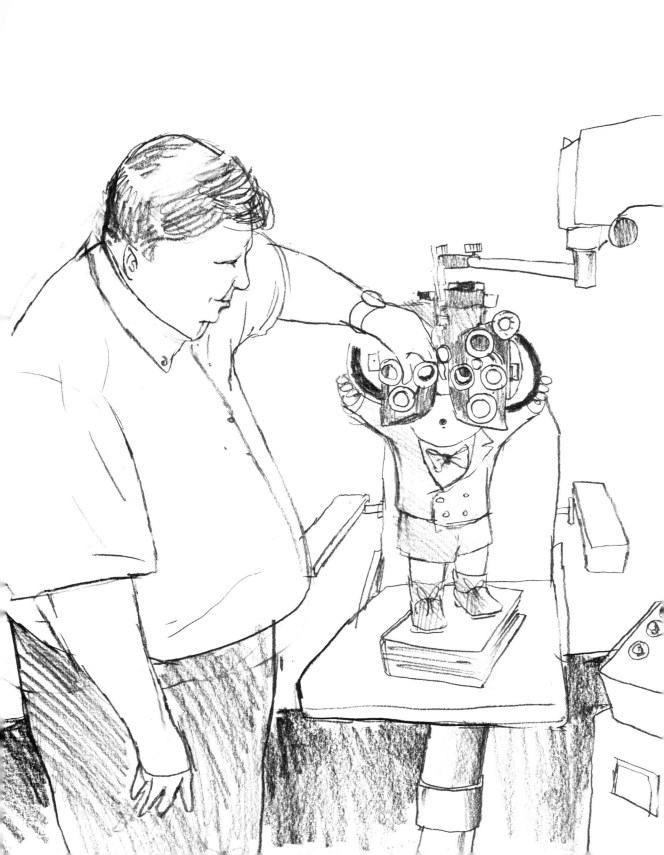

The Burglary

Junior Kroll was caught off guard
When he rounded the house and saw a man in the yard.
Mom was putting the car away.
Jenny the maid was off for the day.
Crazy Max was having his nails done
At the Poochie Palace. Junior broke into a run.
That burglar took off with a sack of loot,
Pursued by the kid in the double-breasted suit.
Junior shouted, "Excuse me, please,"
As he made a lunge for the burglar's knees.
Mrs. Kroll was horrified.
"Junior, let him go!" she cried.
The burglar struggled. Breaking free,
He disappeared beyond the willow tree.
Mrs. Kroll rushed over and brushed off Junior's clothes.
She kissed the tiny beads of sweat on his nose.
But Junior sounded the battle cry,
"Call the cops! I saw that guy."

The Burglary, Part Two

Junior Kroll studied the face
Of Squints McGinty, who began to erase
With the end of a two-inch pencil, then blew
On the paper, dispersing the residue.
It was obvious the sergeant's eyes were bad.
His nose was two inches away from his pad.
He slipped his pencil tip between his lips
And said, "Item two: diamond clips."
"Oops," he said, erasing once more.
Another cop stuck his head through the door,
"Excuse me for interrupting, Squints,
But the guy is here to take fingerprints."
Junior decided that it was time
To assert himself and solve the crime.
"Excuse me, please. I saw his face."
Squints McGinty continued to erase.
"By the time I got there, he was ready to run,"
Said Mrs. Kroll. "I wish I'd had a gun."
Now she had McGinty's attention.
"Mrs. Kroll, I think I should mention,
If you shot him in the back as he left your residence,
You'd be breaking the law because it wasn't self-defense."
Mrs. Kroll dropped her jaw.
"Heaven forbid, I should break the *law*.
He took every piece of my jewelry. I'm so *glad* I let him go.
I might be sitting in a cell right now because I didn't know."
"No need to be sarcastic, Ma'am. I have a job to do.
Okay, diamond clips was item number two."
Junior shot a blast of air
Through his lips and raised his hair.
"I'm telling you, I can pick out that guy.
Show me some mug shots. At least let me try!"

The Burglary, Part Three

Junior Kroll managed to enrage
All the cops as he turned every page
And stared at each face. They hovered around,
Hoping Junior had finally found
The burglar he'd encountered earlier that day
In the middle of making his getaway.
A deathly silence hung over the room.
Then suddenly McGinty began to boom,
"*Well, is that him?*" Junior shook his head.
"That guy's got some haircut," was all he said.
Poor little Junior was unaware
That he was getting into McGinty's hair.
He was, by now, on his fifth mug shot book.
Silently, methodically he continued to look.
Then tapping a photo, "What did *this* guy do?"
McGinty muttered, "Strangled a kid like you."
"Excuse me, sir. What did you say?"
"I said that'll be enough for today."
"I think I should stay till I find
That guy while he's still fresh in my mind."
"You've *seen* every photo. Let's give it up."
Junior drained the Coke from his paper cup.
"If I've really seen everything and there are no more,
He's in book number two on page twenty-four."
"Do you realize," fumed McGinty, "how you've disrupted this place?"
"I just wanted a chance to study the criminal face."

So Junior Kroll helped solve the crime.
They arrested the guy, but he never did time
Because they didn't catch him with the goods,
And he blew the whistle on a few other hoods.

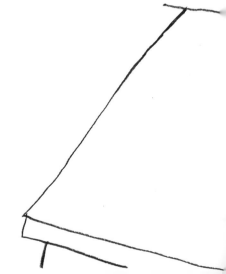

Junior Kroll and the Easter Rabbit

Junior Kroll saved his money
To buy the family an Easter bunny.
He considered milk chocolate and bittersweet,
With solid ears and solid feet.
There were bunnies with baskets of jelly beans
And stylish bunnies wearing tinfoil jeans.
But he couldn't find a bunny just right.
So Junior decided that perhaps he might
Find a bunny of glass or papier-mâché
That would brighten up more than one holiday.
He found bunnies that talked when you pulled their strings
And wind-up bunnies that did crazy things.
But Junior still couldn't make up his mind,
Until the day he happened to find
A bunny on a shelf in an antique store.
And he knew this was the one he'd been searching for.
This bunny was thin, about eighteen inches high.
His fur was all gone and so was one eye.
He had very long legs, and Junior saw
Through the hole in one knee he was stuffed with straw.
The label in his coat read 1933.
He had survived somehow with dignity.
When the family gathered for Junior's surprise,
Mrs. Kroll said an allergy was bothering her eyes.
Grandfather Kroll had to clear his throat,
And Dad kept fussing with the pocket of his coat.
Junior's bunny had touched each heart,
And every year he remained a part
Of the Easter season in the house of Kroll.
A gift from Junior. Bless his soul.

Junior Kroll and His Furry Friend

Junior Kroll is in a hurry.
He just found something green and furry
Making its way across the street
On a zillion little fuzzy feet.
Junior's looking for the Popsicle stick
He threw in the trash. Gotta be quick.
Back to the street, down on his knees.
"Walk up the stick. Hurry now, please.
A little bit more. You're all right."
Up the driveway, hang on tight.
"Hi, Dad! Look what I found."
Junior trips and lands on the ground.

(ENDING ONE:)
There goes the stick, up in the air.
Junior's up. Where, oh where
Is the little green and furry thing?
Lost in the grass. Welcome, spring.

(ENDING TWO:)
There goes the stick, up in the air.
Look at the pretty birdie there.
Where's the green and furry thing?
It's lunch for the birdie; something à la king.

Clean Your Room

"Junior Kroll, clean your room!
Use the dust mop, not the broom.
Get those dust bunnies under the bed.
You'd better get started," Mrs. Kroll said.
She wanted Junior out of the way.
Her Wednesday Garden Club was meeting today.
Up for discussion was the spring cake sale,
When Junior appeared with his arms 'round a pail
Overflowing with dirty socks,
Tootsie Roll wrappers, and a Cracker Jack box.
"I found this stuff under my bed."
The ladies listened; Mom's face turned red.
"Take it to the kitchen and give it to the maid."
"But she always says she's not getting paid—"
That's as far as he got pleading his case,
When the library door closed in his face.
They had just completed plans for the spring cake sale,
When the ladies heard the sound of torrential hail.
Junior poked his head inside the door.
"Excuse me. I spilled my marbles on the floor."
Mrs. Kroll left the library and wilted against the wall.
There were hundreds of marbles all over the hall.
"Pick them up and make it quick.
And what are you doing with that pogo stick?"

"I'm cleaning my *room*!" With his head in his hand,
He snapped his words like a rubber band.
The maid was serving port and tea-rosed petit fours
When suddenly the air outside the French doors
Was filled with flying dust bunnies. The ladies watched them drop.
From an open window above, Junior Kroll shook out his mop.

Taking On Wall Street

Junior Kroll listened to Dad
Telling Grandfather that, though the market was bad,
Perhaps it was time to get back in.
He called it "goin' bottom fishin'."
Junior peeled a Tootsie Roll, settling back to enjoy a good chew
While the financial wizards analyzed *Marty Zweig's Market Review*.
Grandfather wanted dividends; Dad wanted growth.
And Junior wanted to know why they couldn't have both.
But they paid no attention, and Junior Kroll
Amused himself making faces in a silver bowl,
While the two were involved in a heated debate
About capital gains and the interest rate.
Seeing the silver bowl on his head,
They finally listened to what he said.
Junior announced he thought he'd try
Investing his money. He knew what he'd buy.
So Dad placed an order for Totter Construction,
Cyclops Optical, and Cellulite Reduction.
Grandfather purchased Daisy May,
And that trusty old blue chip, Curds and Whey.
But Junior Kroll bought Tootsie Roll,
And much to the others' chagrin,
The broker told them, after the fact,
It was the *only* thing *he'd* be in.

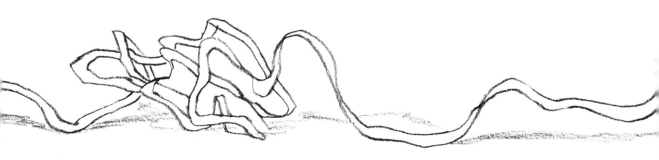

AHOY

Junior Kroll begged to go
Deep-sea fishing but Dad said no.
He was taking clients out for the day
On a chartered boat. There was just no way
They would turn around for a seasick kid.
Though Dad said NO, go Junior did.
It was the roughest sea they'd ever seen.
The sky was gray and the men were green.
Junior Kroll, strapped in his seat,
Had three jelly donuts and was about to eat
An egg salad sandwich when his pole gave a jerk.
The captain said, "Okay, boy. Let's go to work!"
He held Junior, and Junior held the pole.
It was hard to tell for whom the bells would toll.
But Junior got the trophy, and all of you can bet,
Dad had a day he will *never* forget.

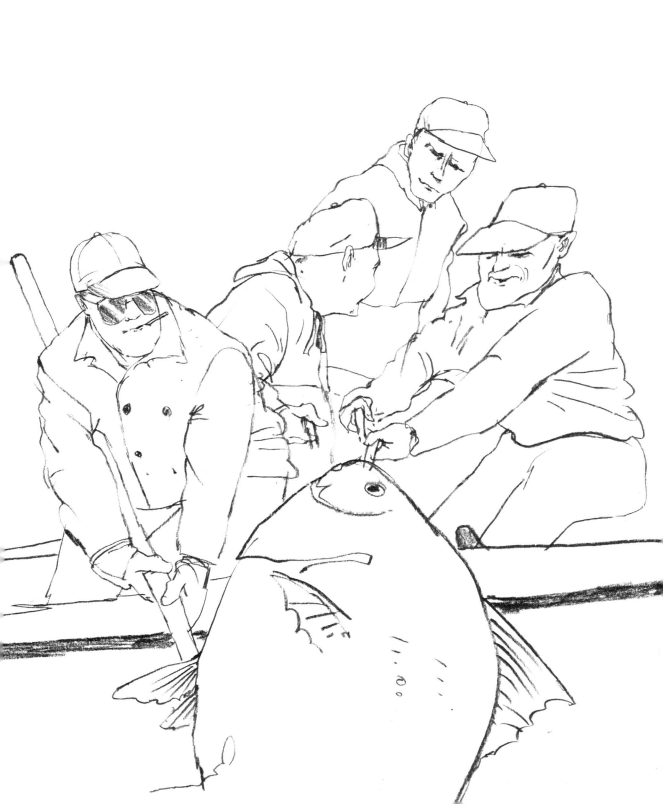

The Lady in the Polka-Dot Shoes

Junior Kroll opened the door
To someone he'd never seen before.
"Iz yaw motha' home, Sugarplum?
I'm an old friend," she added, cracking her gum.
"Who is it, Junior?" he heard Mother call.
"It's a lady chewing gum." Mrs. Kroll reached the hall.
She stared at the stranger, searching the face
That took her back in time to another place.
Best friends they were till the age of ten.
Then they didn't see each other again.
Junior was fascinated by those polka-dot shoes.
He sat listening to the sharing of news,
As the two friends sat and chattered away.
But Junior noticed by the end of Rita's stay,
They had grown quiet. They both just smiled a lot.
Junior, by now, had counted every polka dot.
It was time for good-byes. "You be good, Sugarplum.
You have a wonderful motha'." She cracked that gum.
Mom's eyes were sad. She searched Rita's face,
Remembering a lost friend in a final embrace.
They stood in the doorway waving good-bye,
And Junior Kroll wondered why
Mom said she'd write as soon as she could.
Somehow he knew she never would.

The Bucket o' Bugs

Junior Kroll said, "I beg your pardon,
I'd like a Bucket o' Bugs for my garden.
And is it true that ladybugs provide
The same results as insecticide?"
The salesman explained that ladybugs ate
As many wee pesties as totaled their weight.
So Junior paid the man and headed back,
Eager to launch the big attack.
But he worried about the poor little things,
All scrunched up and longing to spread their wings.
He sat on the curb and raised the lid
Ever so carefully. And when he did,
Whoa! There they go! Must be seven or eight!
Back goes the lid. The rest will have to wait.

At home he placed the bucket on the floor
In the hall in front of the library door.
Then into the kitchen. Now, let's see . . .
Something for lots of energy.
Get the bread, cut off the crust.
Junior sang "It's a Matter of Trust."
Gotta hurry, gotta spread
Mayonnaise on a slice of bread.
Slice of ham, slice of cheese,
"Hello, Max. Excuse me, please.
Get out of the way. I'm not gonna play.
I have to work in my garden today."
As Junior Kroll took a bite,
On went a light bulb, in came the light!
"Oh, no!" He rushed to the library door.
Yes, Max had spilled the Bucket o' Bugs on the floor.
Ladybugs flew all over the room,
Landing on anything that looked in bloom.
Max had a ladybug on the end of his nose.
Three ladybugs sat on a silken rose.
How many were hiding on the oriental rugs?
Poor Junior's left holding the empty Bucket o' Bugs.

The Yard Sale

Junior Kroll hung a sign
At the end of the driveway on the property line:
YARD SALE TODAY—NINE TO FOUR.
By eight the regulars were banging on the door.
With a change maker and a green eyeshade,
Junior was ready, making sure everyone paid.
Mrs. Kroll watched with tears in her eyes
As three little suits and three tiny bow ties
Were snapped up at once and carried away
With a Roly Poly Chicken made of papier mâché.
But Junior Kroll was drunk with power;
He'd made forty-five dollars in less than an hour.
By noon they'd carried off the jelly jars,
Chicken wire, and handlebars,
A bicycle tire, fuzzy dice,
And the remains of a Nerf ball ravaged by mice.
Junior made an emergency call
To Grandfather requesting donations.
Grandfather showed up in no time at all
With mistakes he had purchased on countless vacations.
There was a cowboy hat from a ranch out west,
Itchy wool socks and an itchy wool vest
From County Cork in bright kelly green,
And gaudy T-shirts flaunting the Queen.
The only item left was a round thing
With a crank handle hopelessly stuck.
Nobody could figure out what it was,
But a man took it home for a buck.

Buzz, Buzz, Buzz

Junior Kroll tossed about.
He covered his head but his feet stuck out.
Better find out if the coast is clear.
So he carefully uncovered one little ear.
Oh, no! There it was,
'round and 'round, that relentless buzz.
It was on his foot. He sat up in bed,
Turned on the light. It was a piece of thread.
He rolled up his *Archie* comic book
And stood on the bed for a better look.
This is war. Check each wall.
Whoa, steady now. Don't want to fall.
"What's going on?" It was the voice of doom.
"There's a mutant mosquito in my room."
"Get back in that bed!"
"Oh, please, it's gonna bite."
"You heard what I said, and turn off that light."
"In a minute." He stepped from the bed to the chair.
"Okay, skeeter, say a prayer!"
Wham! *Archie* hit the wall.
The mosquito escaped into the hall.
Junior jumped from the chair to the floor,
Rushed over, and slammed the door.
"What was that? Are you all right?"
"I just closed the door and turned off the light."
Junior hummed a little tune and grinned a little grin.
He got that nasty skeeter out, and it couldn't get back in.

Mrs. Kroll tossed about,
Her head was covered but her feet stuck out.
It was on her foot! She snapped on the light.
A piece of thread? No! A mosquito bite.

Crazy Max and the Battle-Ax

Junior Kroll was worried.
The reason was Crazy Max,
Who was really in trouble this time
For scaring that battle-ax.
She'd been standing in her driveway
When Max decided to pay her a call.
She whacked him with a bag of kitty litter,
And Max didn't like that at all.
He chased her into the woodshed
For a two-hour stay.
She missed her afternoon bridge club
Because he refused to go away.
There had always been a cold war
Between the Krolls and Crazy Max;
But the war now reached the boiling point,
Thanks to that battle-ax.
While Junior pleaded for one more chance,
Max chewed the cuffs on Dad's new pants.
Finally they made up their minds to send him
To stay with Grandfather's cousin Blanche,
Thinking he'd have a lot more freedom
On her Brazilian mahogany ranch.
Junior sat on the verge of tears,
They grew silent in their grief.
Dad stared at the cuffs of his pants,
Shaking his head in disbelief.
Then Max walked in wearing an ice pack.
"What's wrong with him?" Mrs. Kroll said.
"Well, she *hit* him with ten pounds of kitty litter.
He has a big bump on his head."
As Mrs. Kroll swallowed an urge to laugh,
Her shoulders began to shake.
Dad said, "*I* don't think that's funny."
But his indignation began to break.
Soon Mom and Dad were out of control.
"It's okay now, Max," whispered Junior Kroll.

Landing the Big One

Junior Kroll wondered if this was it.
It was twilight when that striper hit.
He stood there remembering what Grandfather had said:
Surf fishing will help you through the years ahead.
It'll teach you patience and feed your soul.
There's just you and the sea and your fishing pole.
But when that striper hits and the battle begins,
You're an angler forever, no matter who wins.
At that moment the pole was almost ripped from his hand,
But he held on tight and landed in the sand.
He was slipping toward the sea still clutching the pole
When someone pulled him to his feet. It was Grandfather Kroll.
He shouted, "You've really hooked a big one. Better give him some line
Or he'll snap that pole in half. Now relax, you're doing fine."
Junior Kroll, drenched to the skin,
Battled that striper and brought him in.
All's well that ends well. Let's give three cheers!
Grandfather has a fish story he'll be telling for years.
The striper's cooked, Junior's hooked,
And everyone sits down to dinner.
There's baked striped bass. Now somebody pass
The peas to Junior, the winner!

The Iron Claw Machine

Junior Kroll was bewitched when he saw
A slot machine with an iron claw
In a belly full of prizes. Something caught his eye;
He must have that genuine purple rabbit's foot or die.
So he fed the beast a dime. He moved the iron claw
And dropped it on the rabbit's foot. But when it started up he saw
The darn thing came up empty. The beast heaved a sigh,
Then went back to sleep; Junior made another try.
He won a flashlight gun, French perfume,
Red velvet lips, a bride and groom,
A tiny toilet to plant your butts,
A package of faded pistachio nuts.
The machine ate up ten bucks in dimes.
And Junior was broke—a sign of the times.

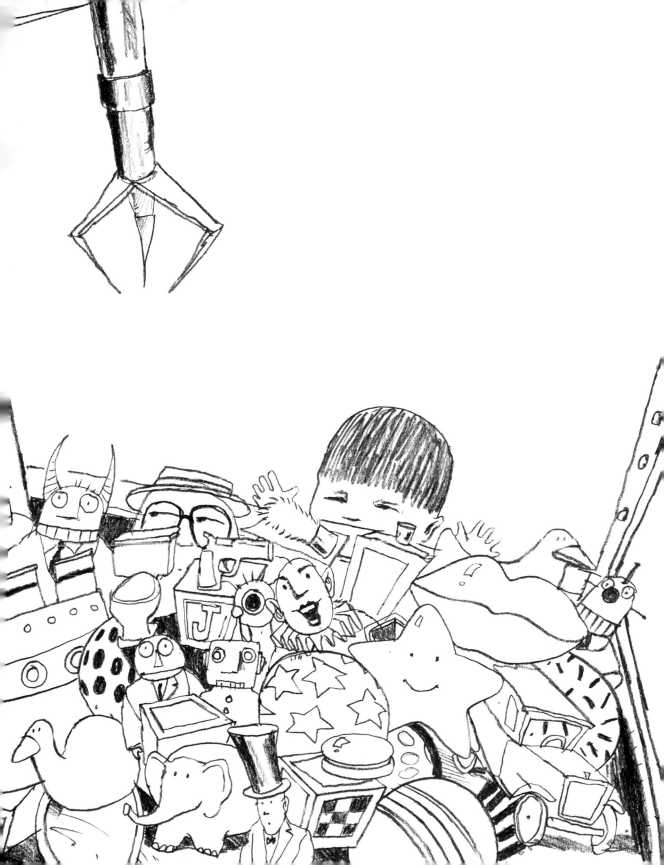

Junior's Prayer

Junior Kroll knelt down to pray.
"Stop it, Max. I'm not gonna play.
Gimme my sock! You heard what I said.
GIMME MY SOCK! Ouch, I bumped my head.
Now, see what you made me do.
Don't you know God is watching you?
Okay, God. Excuse me, please.
It's me, Junior Kroll, down here on my knees.
The other day I was down by the pier,
And there was a sea gull with his leg off to here.
He wasn't crying—just hopping around,
Picking on a french fry he found on the ground.
Then he flew away, and I couldn't understand
How that one-legged sea gull was ever gonna land.
Well, I saw him today. He was hopping along
On his one foot like nothing was wrong,
Right there on Dune Road, and it made me scared
'Cause he was all alone and nobody cared.
So God, if you don't mind now and then,
He could use a little help. Thank you. Amen."

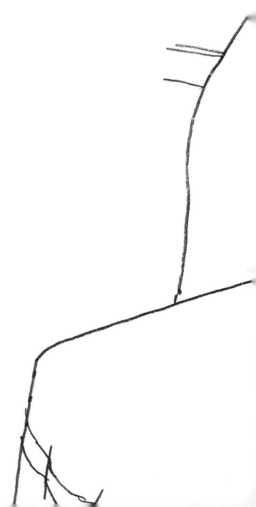

Lance

Junior Kroll gagged on his peas.
With watering eyes he said, "Excuse me, please."
But no one at the table was paying attention.
Their faces were solemn. He heard Dad mention
Mom's cousin Lance and recalled the day
That her cousin, a stranger, arrived from L.A.
He was making a film and looking around
For the right location, but he hadn't found
A place to stay for two weeks or more.
Grandfather graciously opened his door.
The next day Grandfather complained that Lance
Really should have told him in advance
That he was bringing along several of his go-fers.
He also thought Lance was a bit light in the loafers.
But everyone soon had to admit that Lance wasn't bad.
He talked land with Grandfather and law with Dad.
He went shopping with Mom and helped her choose
A gorgeous gown with matching shoes.
Lance was the only one with the patience to play
Tennis with Junior for part of each day.
When he was busy with business they'd anxiously wait
Until he returned. Then they'd all stay up late
To hear the stories he loved to tell,
Hanging on each word for he told them so well.
He widened their world in fifteen short days
And brought them joy in a hundred ways.
And for a while after Lance was gone
The echoes of his laughter lingered on.

It was discovered Lance had AIDS months ago,
Though Mom and Dad thought it best that Junior not know.
"Is Lance coming east?" Junior said.
"No," whispered Mom, "Lance is dead."

Closed for the Season

Junior Kroll stood on the shore.
His nose was stuffed, and his throat was sore.
If he went home he'd be sent to bed,
So he turned and walked up the stairs that led
To the refreshment stand. The sign on the door
Read Closed for the Season. Only two weeks before
Summer hung on. There were people around.
Now there was only the sound
Of the pounding sea. Junior felt sad.
Maybe it was because his throat hurt so bad.
He'd better go home. It was time to move on.
But he knew he felt bad because summer was gone.

The Gospel Beat

Junior Kroll saw a ragged tent,
Heard a gospel beat, and all around was the scent
Of sweet meadow grass. He walked right in.
Up front was a preacher, shoutin' 'bout sin.
The preacher said, "Son, you here to save your soul?"
"I just like the music, sir. My name is Junior Kroll."
And the preacher said, "Sister, give that boy a tambourine."
Junior said, "Excuse me, please," and squeezed in between
A big fat lady with roses on her hat
And a skinny one in purple who had nothing where she sat.
Then a man on the ivories struck a magic chord,
And they all started movin', shoutin', "Praise the Lord."
The tambourines were chingin'. Junior got the beat.
Everyone was singin'; you could hear 'em down the street.
And when the "do" was over and Junior said good-bye,
They asked if he'd come back next week. Junior said he'd try.

Growing Up

Junior Kroll held Grandfather's hand
As they walked the ten-acre tract of land.
They climbed the hill for a better view
And saw a house below and some chickens, too.
Junior pointed to a hawk in the sky,
No bigger than a dragonfly,
Moving closer till they saw his fierce glare.
The hawk was standing in the sky, his wings treading air.
Suddenly he plunged toward the ground.
He was after those chickens. But a man came around
The side of the house, carrying a gun.
That hawk climbed the sky and circled the sun.
He was far away, well out of range,
When Junior saw his direction suddenly change.
The hawk was coming back.
The man began to run.
They heard a thunderous crack.
It was the sound of the gun.
Junior broke away and ran until he found
Where the dead bird lay broken on the ground.
Junior Kroll never said a word,
But he never forgot that fearless bird
With those piercing eyes filled with dust
And the drops of blood that turned the dirt to rust.

The Halloween Follies

Junior Kroll got the leading role in a play about Halloween.
He wore a double-breasted pumpkin suit made of orange velveteen
And a bright green stem on top of his head.
They raised the curtain and Junior said,
 "I'm so glad it's Halloween.
  I'd like to tell you why.
  I'd rather be sittin' on somebody's porch
  Than baked in somebody's pie."
Then he turned around, and when he did,
He collided with another kid.
Down went Junior, up came the sound
Of audience laughter as the pumpkin rolled 'round,
Struggling to rise. But as hard as he tried,
He couldn't get up with his arms stuffed inside.
Mrs. Graves pounded the piano keys, mad as a speckled wet hen,
Playing "Who Blew Out My Candle?" over and over again.
Then a Halloween witch, who was big for her age,
Lifted the pumpkin up from the stage.
Mrs. Graves gave the signal to let the show begin,
As Junior faced the music and gave the crowd a grin.

The Desert Storm

Junior Kroll was eating when
They broke the news on CNN.
He was pushing those peas around his plate,
When the battle started to free Kuwait.
Holliman, Arnett, and Bernard Shaw
Described to viewers what they saw,
As Junior watched with feverish eyes
Those eerie, flashing Baghdad skies.
He fell asleep watching the war.
The next day it wasn't long before
Brokaw and Rather, plus CNN,
Had Junior involved in the battle again.
He picked up the jargon, knew the names and places,
And, amazingly, recognized all the faces.
Mrs. Kroll seemed uneasy and slightly confused.
She suggested he play, but Junior refused.
He cheered the good news; there still wasn't much bad.
Mrs. Kroll's eyes were increasingly sad.
On Friday night, after they ate,
They told Junior there was something that just couldn't wait.
Uncle Tim, a pilot in the Air Force Reserve,
Got his orders to go; he was ready to serve.
Junior didn't watch the news that night.
He went to bed early and left on the light.

Cousin Honey Duff

Junior Kroll's cousin, Honey Duff,
Came to stay with all her stuff.
In minutes Honey found a pair
Of high-heeled shoes and a hat to wear.
The part of Honey Duff between
The hat and the shoes could hardly be seen.
But monkey see, monkey do!
Whatever Junior did, Honey did, too.
Junior said, "Stop it Honey!"
Honey said, "'top it Honey!"
Junior Kroll stuck out his tongue;
Honey did, too, and landed among
The flowers on Mom's hibiscus plant.
"'uner push me," she began to chant.
Mrs. Kroll uprooted Honey's potted behind.
"She made me do it," Junior whined.
Tearfully eyeing each broken bloom
Mrs. Kroll said, "Junior! Go to your room!"
For three long days the war raged on.
Mrs. Kroll's patience was almost gone.
Then Aunt Jane returned for Honey Duff
In her little fur coat and her little fur muff.
They waited for Honey to say good-bye.
But instead, "Wanna stay," she began to cry.
"Oh, pleeeeease!" cried Junior. "Just one more day."
Mrs. Kroll watched Aunt Jane drive away.
And there was Junior trying to teach
His cousin Honey how to reach
The end of her nose with the tip of her tongue.
Poor Mrs. Kroll's nerves were nearly unstrung.
She wondered when her hibiscus would bloom.
Well, not before Junior went back to his room.

Junior Kroll, M.D.

Junior Kroll has lots to do.
Mom and Dad are down with the flu,
And the maid's away, so he's washing clothes.
The washing machine overflows.
Suds are spilling all over the floor.
Up the stairs, open Mom's door.
"Excuse me, please." He breaks the news.
What did he wash? How much soap did he use?
Answer to the first question: dirty socks.
Answer to the second: half the box.
Junior Kroll hears one long groan.
Mom's really sick, better leave her alone.
Dad's in the guest room with pains in his hair.
All he does is move from the bed to the chair.
On his way to the store Junior meets a family friend,
Who asks if his folks are finally on the mend.
Junior tells her they just can't seem to shake the flu.
She takes the time to tell him exactly what to do.

Junior pours a jigger of port into each hot cup of tea.
The friend said it was a sure-cure family recipe.
Then up the stairs he carries the brew on a tray.
The doctor couldn't do it, but Junior saves the day.
Mom and Dad both have seconds. And after a good night's rest,
Dad is reading the *New York Times* and Mom is getting dressed.

Junior Kroll of Scotland Yard

Junior Kroll is proud as punch
In his Sherlock Holmes hat on his way to lunch.
The hat's a gift—not a perfect fit.
It jiggles on his head and itches his eyebrows a bit.
Junior recalls something Grandfather said:
You can tell a lot about a man by the hat on his head.
While waiting for his light to change,
Junior sees a man with a box who's acting very strange.
Could it be the hat affecting his senses?
No! Let's go, Watson. And the chase commences.
Look, he's crossing the street.
Now we must be discreet.
See those mean beady eyes.
That handlebar mustache must be a disguise.
Into the bank! Hat, do your stuff.
Stay back, Watson! We're close enough.
Now, where's the box? He's putting it in
That under-the-counter wastepaper bin.
"Here it is!" Junior's on his knees,
Staring at the box. "Excuse me, please.
Get the police. I believe it's a bomb.
Everybody out! Above all, stay calm."
Is it a bomb? . . . No—it's video cassettes.
Sweatin' to the Oldies, parts one, two, and three.
And *that*, my dear Watson, remains a mystery.

Toys for Needy Girls and Boys

Junior Kroll collected toys
For needy little girls and boys.
Crazy Max, the Krolls' Great Dane,
Pulled the wagon down Beach Plum Lane.
He was supposed to wait while Junior rang each bell,
But that part of the plan didn't go so well.
Poor Max was led astray
By a red Ferrari passing his way.
Then a nosy cat named Cyrano
Tempted fate because he wanted to know
Why Max was doing the job of a horse.
This led to a wild chase, of course.
In spite of the trouble, Junior succeeded,
And dropped off the toys that Santa needed.
But the Devil set a trap in that old church hall.
He was looking for a victim, and Junior took the fall.
In a pile of toys Junior spied
A tiny horse made of real horsehide.
It had soft brown eyes with tiny pinpoints of light.
Junior wanted that horse. But the Devil had to fight.
Junior struggled, then slipped it in his pocket.
The Devil had won. Junior took off like a rocket.

Poor Junior Kroll, riddled with guilt,
Hid the treasure under his quilt.
He must repent. He'd give all his toys
To Santa for the needy girls and boys.
With his conscience eased, Junior closed the door.
His little horse was waiting. He crossed the bedroom floor.
He'd outsmarted the Devil. Junior sat on his bed.
But, alas! The little horse had lost its head.

Junior Kroll and Billy Joel

Junior Kroll saw Billy Joel
Christmas Eve on Newtown Lane,
Holding hands with Christy,
Just walking in the rain.
He followed them 'round the corner,
Into the Country Store;
Junior had seen Billy in concert,
But never in town before.
"Everything's ready," the manager said,
Pointing to packages wrapped in red
Shiny paper with huge green satin bows.
Junior tried to speak but his vocal chords froze.
With four giant shopping bags
The pair crossed the floor.
Junior Kroll rushed ahead
So he could hold the door.
Billy Joel said, "Thank you,"
And patted Junior's head.
Junior watched them cross the street,
Thinking of things he should have said.
Over a hot bowl of soup at O'Malley's
He told Grandfather he couldn't believe
That such a neat thing really happened.
A perfect start to a fine Christmas Eve.

Junior Kroll and the Chocolate Pigs

Junior Kroll saved his nickles and dimes
For presents he wrapped at least fifteen times.
Then he put them all in one big box
Under his bed with his dirty socks.
Junior counted what he had to spend
And divided the total by ten.
The amount was such, he couldn't buy much,
But he came up with a plan in the end.
He bought ten chocolate pigs, a Christmas treat.
Everybody liked something sweet.

It was Christmas Eve, late afternoon.
The family would be arriving soon.
"Wait till they see my presents," he said.
And kneeling down, he reached under the bed.
But his blood ran cold as the shattered box
Slid out on top of his dirty socks.
The pigs were gone. Not even a trace.
Junior knew Max had fallen from grace.

Junior told the story for the fifteenth time
About the chocolate pigs and Max's crime.
And as he told it, the story got longer;
The pigs got bigger, and the laughter grew stronger;
And the Christmas tree lights burned beautiful and bright,
As they shimmered on the snow outside the window all night.